DUMP TRUCKS/
CAMIONES DE VOLTEO

By Katie Kawa   Traducción al español: Eduardo Alamán

 **Gareth Stevens**
Publishing

Please visit our website, www.garethstevens.com. For a free color catalog of all our high-quality books, call toll free 1-800-542-2595 or fax 1-877-542-2596.

Library of Congress Cataloging-in-Publication Data

Kawa, Katie.
Dump trucks = Camiones de volteo / Katie Kawa.
    p. cm. — (Big machines = Grandes máquinas)
English and Spanish.
ISBN 978-1-4339-5580-8 (library binding)
1. Dump trucks—Juvenile literature. I. Title. II. Title: Camiones de volteo.
TL230.15K39 2011
629.224—dc22

                                2011005267

First Edition

Published in 2012 by
Gareth Stevens Publishing
111 East 14th Street, Suite 349
New York, NY 10003

Copyright © 2012 Gareth Stevens Publishing

Editor: Katie Kawa
Designer: Daniel Hosek
Spanish Translation: Eduardo Alamán

Photo credits: Cover and all interior images Shutterstock.com.

Printed in the United States of America

CPSIA compliance information: Batch #CS11GS: For further information contact Gareth Stevens, New York, New York at 1-800-542-2595.

Contents

Contenido

Dump trucks carry things.

Los camiones de volteo llevan cosas de un lado a otro.

Dump trucks have a big box. This is called a bed.

Los camiones de volteo tiene una gran caja. A ésta se le llama cama.

7

Dirt goes in the box.

La tierra va en la caja.

A dump truck gets dirt from a loader.

Una pala cargadora echa tierra en un camión de volteo.

The box tips back.

La caja del camión
se levanta.

13

The box has a door on the back. Dirt comes out of the door.

La caja tiene una puerta en la parte trasera. La tierra sale por la puerta.

In winter, dump trucks carry snow.

En el invierno, los camiones de volteo cargan nieve.

Dump trucks are like cars. They drive on the road.

Los camiones de volteo son como los coches. Se conducen por la carretera.

Dump trucks move on wheels. They can have 18 wheels!

Los camiones de volteo tienen ruedas. ¡Pueden tener 18 ruedas!

The wheels are big.
Some are taller than
a person!

Las ruedas son grandes.
¡Algunas son más altas
que una persona!

Words to Know/
Palabras que debes saber

bed/
(la) cama

door/
(la) puerta

wheel/
(la) rueda

Index / Índice